COUNTRY CROSSING

To my beautiful wife, Donna,
remembering those long ago nights
when we first watched trains together
—J. A.

In memory of my mother, Martha,
who once owned a car like this
—T. R.

COUNTRY CROSSING

by Jim Aylesworth • illustrated by Ted Rand

RAIL ROAD CROSSING

ATHENEUM • 1991 • NEW YORK
Collier Macmillan Canada
TORONTO

Long ago, at a place where a country road
bumped across the tracks, a summer moon softened
the night with quiet light. The moonlight sparkled
in the puddles on the narrow road, and
gleamed like silver on the rails.

Crickets sang softly in the roadside weeds.
Chirp Chirp Chirp Chirrrp
And a lonely owl called from the trees along the tracks.
Hoo Hoo Hoo Hoooooo

Gradually, the sounds of a car stole
into the peaceful night.
　Far away, the old car's motor went,
　Puttaputt putt putt putt.
　Puttaputt putt putt putt.
　The tires went,
　Churrrrrr,
as they rolled along the pavement.
　With pale headlights searching out
the road ahead, the car came nearer and nearer.
The sounds grew louder and louder.

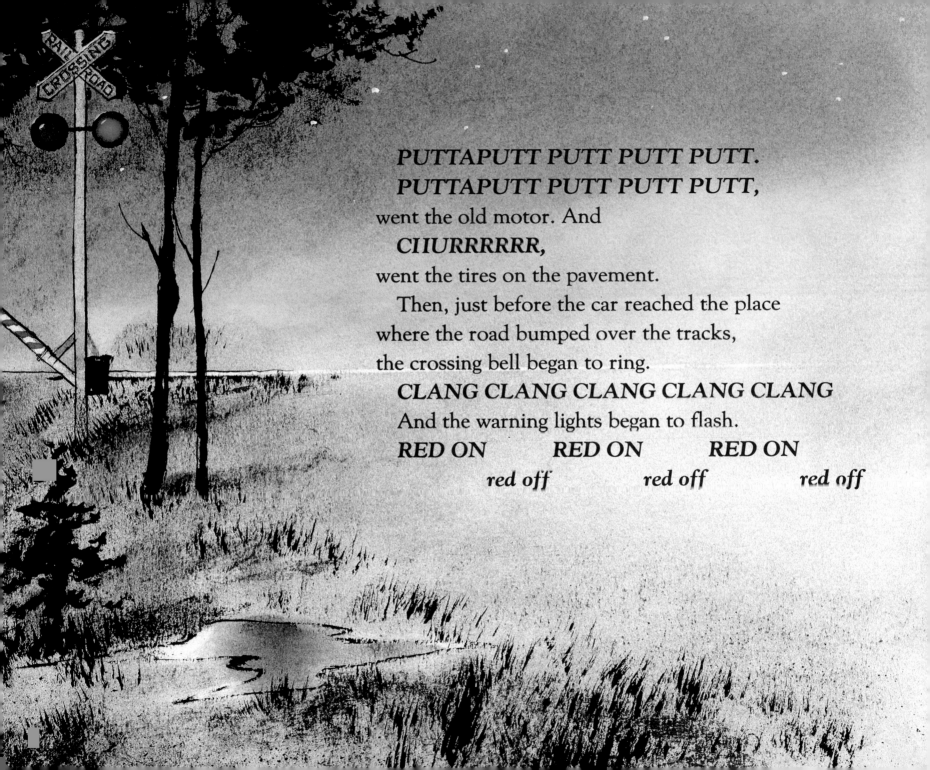

PUTTAPUTT PUTT PUTT PUTT.
PUTTAPUTT PUTT PUTT PUTT,
went the old motor. And
CHURRRRRR,
went the tires on the pavement.

Then, just before the car reached the place
where the road bumped over the tracks,
the crossing bell began to ring.
CLANG CLANG CLANG CLANG CLANG
And the warning lights began to flash.
RED ON   RED ON   RED ON
red off   red off   red off

The old car slowed,
splashed through a moonlit puddle,
SPLISSHHHH,
and came to a stop.
The crossing bell rang.
CLANG CLANG CLANG CLANG CLANG
And the warning lights flashed.
RED ON   RED ON   RED ON
red off   red off   red off

Soon, a train whistle rose in the distant night.

Whooawoo

Whooawooooooo

And as the old car waited, a strong yellow light
began to poke its way through the trees,
and the roar of an engine began
to rumble out of the darkness.

Chooachoo choo choo choo

Chooachoo choo choo choo

Chooachoo choo choo choo

And then it was there...like a giant roaring!
CHOOACHOO CHOO CHOO CHOO
CHOOACHOO CHOO CHOO CHOO
WHOOAWOO WHOOAWOOOOOO

Speeding! Steel wheels racing on the rails!
Yellow light searching! Smoke pouring into the sky!

Sparks flying! Dead leaves whirling!
Weeds bending in the wake! The engine sped through the night.

The crossing bell rang.

CLANG CLANG CLANG CLANG CLANG

And the warning lights flashed.

RED ON   **RED ON**   **RED ON**

red off   *red off*   *red off*

Then freight car after freight car followed the giant into the night.
The headlights of the waiting car shone upon their wheels.
CLICKITY CLACK CLICKITY CLACK
CLICKITY CLACK CLICKITY CLACK

On and on they raced. Freight car after freight car.
Ten after ten. Tank cars. Flat cars.
Orange after orange. Black after black.
**CLICKITY CLACK CLICKITY CLACK
CLICKITY CLACK CLICKITY CLACK**

And the old car waited. And the crossing bell rang.
CLANG CLANG CLANG CLANG CLANG
And the warning lights flashed.
RED ON   RED ON   RED ON
  red off   red off   red off

At last came the caboose. It passed with a rush and a swirl of dust.
A leaf flew into the air, then skidded to a stop across the road.

Slowly the sound of the train began to slip away.
The roaring of the engine got fainter and fainter.
The clickity clacking of the wheels got softer and softer.
The whistle sounded far, far away.

Whooawoo

Whooawoooooo

Soon the sounds of the train were gone...
all swallowed by the night.
The crossing bell stopped ringing.
The warning lights stopped flashing.
And the old car was left alone.

After a moment, the car lurched slightly,
bumped across the tracks and, like the train,
began to fade into the night.
The old motor got fainter and fainter.
The churring of the tires got softer and softer.
The taillights got dimmer and dimmer. And then,
they, too, were gone...all swallowed by the night.

The night became as peaceful as before.
The moonlight sparkled in the puddles
on the narrow road and gleamed
like silver on the rails.
Crickets sang in the weeds.
Chirp Chirp Chirp Chirrrp

And from the trees, a lonely owl
called out into the summer night.
Hoo Hoo Hoo Hooooooooo